THE FLIGHTS *of* MARCEAU

RACE TO THE RESCUE

by **JOE BROWN** • *illustrated by* **STEPHEN MARCHESI**

Scholastic Inc.

New York Toronto London Auckland

Sydney Mexico City New Delhi Hong Kong

Based on an original idea by Maxx and Gabe Fisher

To my grandchildren; my daughter Bobbi, who restarted my motor;
and to my best friend, Lola, who also happens to be my wife
(How lucky am I?)
— J. B.

ISBN-13: 978-0-545-13473-6
ISBN-10: 0-545-13473-0

Text copyright © 2009 by Joe Brown
Illustrations copyright © 2009 by Stephen Marchesi

12 11 10 9 8 7 6 5 4 3 2   13 14 15 16/0

Printed in the U.S.A. 113
First printing, November 2009

Marceau is my name and I'm driving a cab.

And my imagination helps me to escape from the **drab**.

For the world as I know it is tired and dry,

But my mind lets me fly to the **heights** of the sky.

---

drab - dull, boring   **heights** - top

Now my young **fare**, let's get on our way,
To drop you at school as I do every day.
Sit back and relax, I've a story for you
About **terrified** animals in a poor, troubled zoo.

---

fare - taxi passenger   **terrified** - scared

Afraid of the **hurricane** coming their way,

Most people had left from New Orleans that day.

They had to leave and everyone was sad.

But they had no choice—the weather was too bad.

---

hurricane - a huge storm with powerful winds

The zoo in the city was left unprotected,
with all of the animals badly **neglected**.
A **torrential rain** soon covered the zoo.
The **panicking** animals didn't know what to do.

---

neglected - not cared for   **torrential rain** - a sudden rush, downpour
panicking - very scared

Their nerves had been **frayed**; their senses were **heightened**—
They had every right to be very frightened.
With no one around, the zoo was forgotten.
The food got wet and began to turn rotten.

---

frayed - worn down   **heightened** - raised

They all were locked up inside of their cages,
And none had been out of those cages in **ages**.

---

ages - a long time

I had very little time to be wasting that day—
I had to get to the zoo by the fastest way!

But the winds were so strong from the hurricane
That no one could fly in an airplane.
Those winds were so strong, though it seems quite **absurd**,
It was not even safe on the wings of my bird.
It was silly to think about going by train,
Since all of the bridges washed out in the rain.
The only way there was over the land—
But not by the roads, which were covered with sand.

_____

absurd - silly

Of course! I thought of a perfect plan
That would involve the swiftest animal known to man.
The fastest of the fastest is a feline named Rita,
Known far and wide as the world's fastest cheetah.
She came at my signal, just as quick as a wink.
I explained my **dilemma**, and she started to think.

———————————
dilemma - problem

"You can get on my back and we'll ride like the wind,
But there's a problem," she said, looking **chagrined**.
"I can only run one hundred miles, I fear,
And the zoo is a thousand miles from here.

chagrined - worried, upset

"In order for us to achieve success
I would race to the rescue like the **Pony Express**."
In early America what they needed most
Was a way to get mail from coast to coast.
The mail had to get through, and many had tried,
But the distance was too great for one horse to ride.
It was a job for many, not only for one,
So they kept changing horses 'til the journey was done.

___

Pony Express - mail delivery system in the West in the 1880s

It would require great effort to **accomplish** our ends,
So Rita sure helped when she gathered her friends!
Nine other cheetahs, spread out from the start,
Would be waiting one hundred miles apart.

———————————

accomplish - succeed

Can you even imagine the problems involved?
There were mountains of problems that had to be solved.
Like when I finally got there, what would I do?
The animals *all* needed food, not just a few.
Getting food to the hungry would be a great **feat**,
Because I didn't even know what most of them eat.
Some would need meat and some would need hay,
But whatever they'd need, they'd need right away.

feat - great deed

We prepared to use the sun as our guide.
At the dawn of that day we started to ride.
We went one hundred miles in two hours flat.
I couldn't believe the great speed of that cat!
It all came together as **anticipated**.
At every new station, a fresh cheetah waited.

---

anticipated - expected

Through thickets and grasslands and rivers we breezed,
And arrived there by morning, feeling tired but pleased.
By mysterious means we put out the word
From animal to animal and bird to bird.
The elephants brought food that elephants eat,
While the lions and tigers brought **succulent** meat.
The eagles brought prey, and as I **recall**,
The camels brought plenty of water for all.

succulent - juicy   **recall** - remember

Helping so **noble** an effort, I thought,
Was a feeling of value that could not be bought.
The animals ate; it was a sight to behold—
Worth much more to us than diamonds or gold.

——————

noble - admirable

I knew I couldn't describe in words
The grateful songs being sung by the birds.
Before the day was over, we'd fed quite a few,
Like the wolf and the hippo and the kangaroo.

We fed egrets and polar bears, each white as vanilla.
There were bananas galore for the amazing gorilla.
They brought branches for the **endangered** okapi,
And food for the monkeys, who proved a bit sloppy.

———————————————
endangered - almost extinct

You can tell that our journey was very worthwhile,
Just ask the rhino, the zebra, or crocodile.
The giraffes had been fed and the chimpanzee, too.
Happiness, at last, had returned to the zoo.

They cheered and they roared and I have to confess
That the feeding of the animals was a great success.
The waters **receded**; the keepers returned,
Never to forget the lesson they learned.
From now on the food would be stored with great care
So when it was needed, it would surely be there.

receded - went down

These stories that I tell to you are not rare events,
When I use my imagination, it always makes sense.
I admit they're not fact, but just how I feel.
While driving my cab they appear very real.
My adventures are filled with great joy and sorrow—
If you want to hear more . . . just tune in tomorrow!